CONTENTS

Original Fairy Stories by
Johanna Spyri, Hans Christian Andersen,
Charles Perrault and others.
Translated and Retold by
LILY OVEN

Brown Watson
(Leicester) Ltd

Illustrations Copyright © MCMLXXX by Lito Publishers
English text Copyright © MCMLXXX by Brown Watson
Published in Great Britain by Brown Watson
55a London Road, Leicester LE 2 OPE
All rights reserved throughout the world
Printed in Czechoslovakia
ISBN 0 7097 0148 9
50200/51/05

My Wonderful World of

FAIRY TALES

The Travels of Pipo

WINTER was coming near. Mr. and Mrs. Squirrel were busy gathering in a store of food to eat during the cold weather.

"Come along now, Pipo," they said to their youngest child. "You must help, too, like your brothers and sisters, or you will have nothing to eat when the winter comes. Then what will you do? You will be very sorry for all this idleness."

But Pipo paid no heed. He was very young and didn't like work. He wanted to play all the time, and make his brothers and sisters laugh, and get into mischief and just do what he liked. He also liked to eat, sleep, and dream.....

He specially liked dreaming, and usually he dreamed of travelling. Oh, to travel! To go off and discover the World! He was sure the World was a beautiful place, where everything was easy and gay and wonderful.

And one night, when everything was quiet and still in the home, and everyone was sleeping, Pipo woke up and suddenly made a great decision. He would go off and discover the World!

There and then he got together some things he might need and tied them up into a large spotted handkerchief. Then he put on his hat, took a last look at his brothers and sisters all sleeping, and climbed out through the window.

With one leap he landed on the moss at the foot of the tree where he lived. The jump hurt his soft paws a little, but who cared about that! He was free, and long live freedom!

Which way should he go? Straight ahead, of course, along the track shining in the moonlight. But the track was stony and hurt his feet. Perhaps freedom was a little dangerous!

Then a voice called out: Pipo! Where are you going at this time of night?"

It startled him, but he recognised Mrs. Weasel suddenly standing there.

"Oh, Mrs. Weasel, you frightened me! I am off to discover the World! But don't speak so loudly – I don't want anyone to know."

"And exactly what do you mean?" she demanded.

"Well, you know, I'm going travelling – to visit far off lands, meet people and other animals – all that sort of thing."

"And you are going to do all this alone?" she asked.

"Of course! I am quite big enough now. But – I must get along."

"I suppose you've thought of all the sorrow you will cause your family? Your poor mother will weep when she finds your empty bed to-morrow."

"Ah – well – no, I hadn't thought of that. But it will be all right. Perhaps you will give her my love, and tell her that I shall come back one day, very rich and famous and grand. Good-bye, Mrs. Weasel."

"Good-bye, Pipo! Take good care of yourself, and come back soon. Your friends will be waiting for you."

Off he went, whistling to keep up his courage, because the forest was full of strange night noises. Somewhere an owl hooted. Over there Master Fox lurked around. Bats kept swooping around. He had never known that the forest was so busy and noisy at night. He couldn't see quite so well, either, for a cloud had drifted over the moon.

In fact, he didn't feel quite so brave.

Suddenly, close by him, there came a loud mournful cry that made him jump.

"Whoo-hoo! Whoo-hoo!"

It frightened him to death!

He stopped, pricked up his ears, then stammered:

"Wh-wh-what do you want? Who is it?"

"Ha, ha, ha!" laughed the voice. "You little rascal! Of course you know me!"

Of course he did. It was only the wise old forest owl.

He replied: "Oh, it's you, sir. I – er – I'm just off on my way. I'm going to discover the World."

"Whoo-hoo . . . hmm . . . aren't you a little young for such things? Don't you know that there are all kinds of dangers out there? Winter is coming, and when the snow falls, you won't be able to find any kind of nuts to eat. And like all great travellers, you won't have a comfortable home to come back to at night, when the icy north winds are blowing and wolves are out looking for prey. Not to mention the cold."

"You sound very pessimistic, Mr. Owl. I am very sorry, but I must hurry off because I want to get to the end of the world. Good-bye."

Once more he was alone and now the night was black, for the moon had disappeared. And he was sleepy. He stumbled along the track, thinking he would like to rest for a few hours.

Suddenly he came to a large tree, with a thick mossy carpet around its roots, and he stopped. He would rest here, he decided. He snuggled down into the moss and was soon fast asleep.

He dreamed, of course, this time of gorgeously coloured birds who kept trying to persuade him to fly off with them.

"I would like to, but I have no wings," he said, and with that he woke up, to find the sun shining, the forest full of chirpings, and real birds flying all around him.

"I say, why are you making all this noise?" he asked, looking around him.

"Because we are happy, little squirrel! The sun is shining and it's warm!"

"Oh, is that all? You've wakened me up and I was so tired! I'm on my way to discover the World and it's very hard work!"

"Discover the World! Ha-ha – what a funny thing to do! Don't you like it here in the forest, with your friends and family?"

"Of course I do, but it is exciting to discover the World! And now I'm getting hungry, and it's your fault for wakening me."

But the whole forest was waking up. One by one a family of baby rabbits came out to play and dance on a stretch of grass.

Pipo watched them. Oh, how he would love to play with them!

But he was getting more and more hungry. He got up, searched around and found a few acorns, then put on his hat, flung his stick and his bundle over his shoulder, and set off again.

Some hours later he arrived at an immense lake. A large duck came swimming up to him.

"Can I help you? I am Caroline, and it is my job to carry travellers to the other side of the lake. I only charge a few pence."

"Yes, please," said Pipo, though he had no money at all.

And he climbed on to her back and settled down comfortably as Caroline swam off across the lake, making for the other side.

Caroline was very talkative and soon began telling the latest gossip of the lake.

"Some swans arrived yesterday – you should have heard the noise of their wings. They're staying a few days before they go off to the mountains," she said.

"So!" thought Pipo. "I'm not the only one who likes to travel."

"And Mrs. Hen has at last hatched her eggs. Eight lovely little downy chickens have been born," said Caroline.

On and on she went with her chatter, till he was weary of it, and wished she would stop.

Then he had an idea. He would catch some fish!

He tied some thread to his stick, and a hook to the thread, then dangled it in the water, where it bobbed around a little. Then suddenly it became tight and he could feel something pulling on it . . .

"Hurrah!" he screamed. "I've caught a fish!"

He pulled up the line, and sure enough a plump little fish dangled from it.

"Ho, ho!" he sang. "What fun! It's my lucky day to-day – oh, this is the life! Now I'll catch another fish, and then another, and then – – "

He threw back the line, but this time nothing happened. This time he was not lucky, and he soon began to get bored.

Caroline the duck didn't say anything, but laughed to herself. She knew there were very few fish in the lake, in fact.

But now they were near the shore of the lake. He threw away his line and hook, and scrambled off Caroline's back and up the bank.

But now he had to confess, looking very ashamed, that he had no money to pay for his trip, but he would come back one day, he said, and bring Caroline a fine present.

"Oh, that's all right," she said. "I'll just take the fish you've caught." And she grabbed it out of his paw and swam off.

Oh, well, it didn't matter. At least he was on the other side of the lake. And he set off, swaggering, to find the World.

But now he was very hungry again, so he began to search around for a few more acorns to eat. Suddenly, a most lovely scent drifted to him. He sniffed hard.

"Mmm – that smells good! Now where does it come from?" he thought.

Pipo looked all around but could find nothing. He searched among the bushes, but still nothing. Feeling more and more hungry, he then climbed up the trunk of a large tree – and there he came upon two bees, who seemed very busy.

"Good morning. I am Pipo the squirrel," he said politely.

"Pipo who?" asked the bees.

"The SQUIRREL!"

"Oh. Good morning to you."

"What are you doing?" he asked.

"We are gathering the juice from the flowers and putting it into this little pot."

"Oh. Is that what smells, then? Why are you gathering it? What is it for?"

"You are very curious, Pipo, but we shall tell you since you are at least polite. With the juice of the flowers, we make honey."

"Honey? And is it good to eat?"

"Of course it is! All the children adore it!"

"Would you give me a little, then?"

"Sorry, but we can't do that, squirrel, because the flower juice is very precious." They began fluttering their wings. "And anyway, we have to go now, back to the hive. Our queen is expecting us. Come and see us sometime, and then we'll let you taste the honey."

And off they flew.

"Well, the mean, heartless creatures!" said Pipo. "Work, work, work, and can't spare a minute to help me!"

He felt very angry and ran down to the ground. But there he saw an amazing sight. A great number of ants were slowly walking along, one behind the other, each one carrying a load many times larger and heavier than herself.

"What courage! What strength!" thought Pipo. "I don't think I could do that. But surely they will help me."

He hardly liked interrupting them, but he must find something to eat. So after a minute he said: "Excuse me, ladies, but could you stop a minute and listen to me? I am very, very hungry. If you could lend me just a few of your berries, I will pay them back. Oh, do please help me."

But they simply marched on, though their king, who was with them, stopped a minute and explained to Pipo that they were getting ready for the winter, which was very near and which was going to be hard.

"And you should follow our example," he told Pipo. "If you don't want to die of starvation when the winter comes."

Then he hurried off after his army.

Well, as he was a king he was probably very wise, thought Pipo, but really, to discover the World was far more important than preparing for the winter, whatever that might be.

Poor Pipo! He could find no help at all. But he set his teeth and promised himself that he would never give up, no matter what happened, till he had conquered the World and found a fortune.

He didn't notice at first a lot of tiny white flakes floating around in the air.

Then a larger one landed on his little nose and he looked up. He blew hard to send it away, but it just stayed there and began to melt on his nose.

Oh goodness! What was happening?

Of course Pipo was only a few months old. He didn't know what winter was, except something that folks were always talking about.

And suddenly it felt very cold. But then he began chasing the snowflakes, and the exercise made him feel a lot warmer, although he was still very, very hungry. Oh, where could he find something to eat?

Suddenly a sort of ball struck him and whirled him round and round, till he was quite dizzy, and almost fell. When he got his balance, he saw that the ball had straightened itself out into a mole, who stood there panting and weeping bitterly.

"Oh, my babies!" she wept. "The snow eagle has picked them up and flown off with them to his nest, which is at the top of the highest tree in the forest!"

And she dragged Pipo into her hole and told him all about this terrible thing.

Pipo, very shocked, immediately offered to get them back, because poor Mrs. Mole was so unhappy. Great tears ran down her face and made a puddle on the table, until at last Pipo interrupted her grief to say that he was very hungry and would like something to eat before setting out to rescue her babies. There was a fine appetising smell in the kitchen.

Mrs. Mole dried her tears, laid the table, and lost no time in serving the tasty food which had been simmering away on the fire.

"Mmmm – Mrs. Mole is a good cook," thought Pipo, eating hungrily, at last.

Then he put on his hat, and poked his nose outside.

Now the snow was falling in great flakes, making a thick white carpet over everywhere, which crunched under his paws, when he tried to walk on it.

"Oh, you are so brave, Pipo!" cried Mrs. Mole. "I know you will rescue my babies, but take care of yourself, won't you? You needn't be afraid of the cold. Good-bye, then! See you soon, I hope."

Carefully Pipo set off, sinking into the snow with every step but leaving fine big footprints behind him, which he thought were very pretty.

After a while he became more sure of himself, taking little slides and even somersaults, which made him all white. It was fun, but he knew he mustn't spend too much time playing about, because Mrs. Mole's babies were in great danger. He knew that the eagle was very wicked, and he just hoped he would arrive in time to save the baby moles.

Pipo had plenty of sense, even though he was so very young, and already his travels had taught him a lot. So he soon found out where the eagle's nest was. It was very high indeed!

Fortunately, the eagle had gone off in search of more prey. Pipo began to climb up the trunk of the great fir tree. Of course this was easy for him, as he lived in trees, and was just like a game.

When he reached the nest, he crept up carefully so as not to frighten the baby moles, who were trembling and crying with fear.

"Don't be afraid," he told them when at last he reached them. "I am a friend of your mother's and I have come to rescue you. But we must hurry!"

Carefully he carried first one, then the other baby, down the tree and set them on the snow. "Oh!" he thought. "I never thought I'd find myself rescuing baby moles! Travel certainly broadens the mind, as the proverb says. Yes – everybody should travel! Long live freedom!"

The two baby moles were almost stupefied after their terrible adventure, but very glad to be rescued, so they tried not to cry.

And now Pipo did a strange thing. He rolled them over and over in the snow, like fish being dipped in flour for cooking, until they were all white and the eagle would not be able to see them if he came looking for them.

Mrs. Mole was overjoyed when two fat little white balls came bouncing towards her, though she could only recognise their noses and feet.

"Oh, my babies! You are safe!" she cried. "Thank you very much, Pipo! You are the bravest squirrel I have ever known. I shall never forget this!"

And she went to the door and called out: "Everybody – come at once! We are going to give a great feast for the brave Pipo!"

And in less time than it takes to say, she had started preparing a party, helped by her neighbour Mrs. Weasel.

She made heaps of blackberry tarts, delicious jams, and great jugs of blackcurrant syrup.

The news had spread quickly. Animals arrived from all over the forest, and when they heard what Pipo had done, they all cheered loudly, and told Pipo what a fine fellow he was, and how they were all afraid of the wicked eagle.

Then they settled down to eat all the good things Mrs. Mole offered them.

The birds brought pretty sprays of berries to decorate the underground home of the moles.

The rabbits' orchestra tuned up their instruments and played gay tunes all night long, for the guests to dance to. Mrs. Mole kept on bringing more food to set out on the table, and the guests kept on eating it.

Pipo was very proud of himself, but he couldn't help feeling a little shy at all this fuss. He tried to hide himself in a corner, but a robin redbreast found him and dragged him out by the ear.

"What's the matter with you?" he demanded. "Don't you feel happy amongst us?"

"Oh, yes, yes!" replied Pipo. "But . . . but . . . "

"You must stay here forever!" said Mrs. Mole, firmly.

"Oh, yes, Pipo, do stay!" cried everyone, all together.

"But – but – " said Pipo.

"We will make a lovely home for you!" said a rabbit. "And we will line it with our fur, so that it will always be warm."

"We will get some branches from the oak tree and make a comfortable bed and a table and chairs," said Mr. Badger.

"And I will knit you a big warm pull-over and a pair of cosy red slippers," said Mrs. Badger, and right away she produced her knitting needles, ready to start at once.

"No – come and live with me up in the mountains," said a fine young deer. "It is magnificent up there, especially in winter. And the air is so good and pure – once you have lived there you will never want to come back to the forest."

"You are all so good, and so kind, and truly I would like to stay with you," said Pipo, suddenly weeping a little. "But I . . . I want to go home. I want to see my parents and my brothers and sisters. I haven't seen them for such a long time."

"Of course, of course," said Mrs. Mole kindly. "But we shall have to help you, Pipo, because the snow is now very deep and hard. Everybody – go and bring your spades and pickaxes, and we will clear a road for Pipo!"

And very soon everyone was working away as hard as possible, clearing a path for Pipo to go home.

They pushed and argued and quarrelled a little, but always Mrs. Mole was there to set things right. And of course there

were one or two small accidents – a torn ear or a cut foot, but there again Mrs. Mole consoled the little sufferer and soothed away his tears.

At last they had hacked their way out of the hole, and it was time to say good-bye. And Pipo was very sad indeed to leave all these good friends with whom he had so much enjoyed himself.

He cuddled the two baby moles, and told them to be very careful in future not to go away from their mother.

"We won't," they said. "And we shall never forget how you saved us from the terrible claws of the forest eagle."

"Good-bye, Mrs. Mole," said Pipo then. "I will come and see you again next spring, and bring my parents and brothers and sisters, who will be very glad to meet you."

And now he set off towards home. They all watched him till he had disappeared round a bend in the road.

It was going to be a long way ahead before he reached his family's cosy nest.

But now he felt very unhappy. What would his mother say? What would his father say? Pipo had gone off so suddenly, and such a long time ago. But surely they would forgive him, because surely they loved him very much!

After he had walked a very long way, he saw a tree which looked familiar. His heart began to beat quickly. Softly he drew near . . . . . and then he saw his parents! He leapt towards them and hugged them.

"Oh, Pipo, we thought we had lost you forever!" wept his mother.

"Young rascal!" growled his father.

But already Pipo was playing with his brothers and sisters, and didn't hear what his parents were saying.

Yes, everyone was glad to see him, and kept offering him all kinds of good things to eat.

Then Mrs. Squirrel made a bed for him.

And when he was in it, he thought that even if he had not conquered the World, he had found out how good it was to have a home, and how necessary it was to work.

Then he decided he was going to stay here and sleep till the spring came, and he closed his eyes.

The Little Match Girl

ONCE upon a time, in the country of Denmark, there lived a little girl, whose parents had both died. She was not very unhappy at first, because she went to live with her grandmother, who looked after her very well. But after only a few months the old lady also died, and now the little girl was left, all alone, in the attic room where her grandmother had lived.

Also, she had to buy food. All she had was a tray full of boxes of matches, for she had helped her grandmother by selling matches on the streets.

She had had a very bad cold and couldn't leave the house, but now it was Christmas Eve, and she must go out to try and sell some matches, so that she could get money to buy a little food.

It was bitterly, bitterly cold. She had no shoes and her clothes were not warm. Soon her feet felt frozen, but she told herself that surely someone would buy a few boxes of matches, especially as it was Christmas Eve.

"Please buy my matches to light your candles and make your Christmas tree look pretty," she begged.

But there was an angry, whistling wind that carried her voice away, and in any case there were very few people on the streets. Because the winter had come early that year, they had done their Christmas shopping weeks ago, and now they were all warm and cosy indoors, getting ready for their Christmas feasting and fun.

In fact she could see them, behind the brightly lit windows of the houses, which were so prettily outlined with white snow. Fires were burning in large fireplaces, and she guessed they were giving out much warmth. The whole town seemed to be ready for Christmas, all except her.

She felt that her heart was broken as she wandered along through the town, shivering in her rags.

Now and again she stopped in front of a closed door and called out in a small voice: "Does anybody want to buy any matches?"

No one heard her, of course. Everyone was busy inside those closed doors, watching the children playing with their new toys, opening presents wrapped up in brightly coloured paper, eating delicious food spread out on large tables, all decorated with flowers, pretty china and silver.

The match-seller knew very well what it would be like inside the houses. Not long ago she too had been a very happy little girl, spoiled by her parents. She too had had lots of wonderful Christmas presents. Now, her heart ached as she remembered those happy times.

"If only my grandmother could have stayed," she thought to herself. "Even though our room was poor we were happy together, Grandmother making the lace cloths which the rich

ladies bought. And I decorated the boxes of my matches with my coloured crayons and people bought those, too. But now my crayons are used up, my paint brushes worn out, and even my paints have become hard and useless."

She felt very frightened. What was to become of her?

Pulling her shawl closer around her shoulders, the little girl wandered on around the streets, hardly knowing where she was going, or what she was doing, she was so cold and hungry.

Three times she thought she saw someone in the distance, and ran after them full of hope.

But the first time what she thought might be a customer turned out to be a tree whose branches were waving about in the wind.

The second time it was nothing but a snowman at the corner of the street. He just stood there, not minding the snow, and not caring about her, either.

But the third time it really was a man, walking quickly along . . . she could hear his footsteps . . she hurried after him.

He stopped outside a door and began to bring out his key.

"Sir, sir!" she cried, coming up to him. "Please, sir, will you buy some matches from me?"

The man, who was well muffled up a thick fur cape, turned as he heard her and stared, frowned at her angrily and said: "Be off with you!"

He waved her away, opened his door and went in. And just for a moment she saw brightness and heard laughter. Then the heavy oak door slammed in her face, and she was alone again in the cold and darkness.

She turned away in despair, and went and sat down in a corner, pressing her arms around herself to try and make herself less cold.

Once more the street was empty and silent except for the cruel wind, which shrieked louder and cut through the little girl.

Little by little she could feel herself going to sleep, and struggled hard to keep awake, for she knew it was very dangerous to fall asleep in the snow. She had heard stories of explorers to the North Pole. A terrible white sleep could overcome them and once they fell in the snow, it covered them and they were lost forever.

Now what could she do? Where could she go? What was going to happen to her? The way back to her attic room was long, and her legs felt too numb to take her there. In any case she didn't want to go. It was an ugly room. She had only been happy there because her grandmother had been with her.

Suddenly she had an idea. She couldn't sell her matches, so she would use them to get herself warm!

At first her stiff fingers refused to strike the matches, and she wasted quite a number of them, because they broke and fell to the ground.

Weeping at all this waste, she tried again, and at last succeeded. A weak little flame trembled in the winter wind. She put her hand round it to protect it, and it seemed to grow into a great golden light.

"Oh, this is lovely!" she whispered, and in the light, her white cheeks seemed to become a little more rosy.

But after only a moment, the match became all black and charred and went out.

So she opened another box and struck several all at once.

Oh, what a wonderful flame they made! She could actually feel their warmth, it seemed to warm all her body. And it made her think of long summer days in bright sunshine which she had spent at the seaside. There was sand, warmed by the sun, soft and smooth under her bare feet.

The whole world was full of this glorious warmth! Any minute now, she thought, the clock would strike dinner time; there would be apple tart and sweet honey on the table to eat . . . .

Then she gave a great shiver as the light grew dim and fizzled out and again there was only the cold and the wind and the darkness all around her.

"The light of a match doesn't last very long," she said to herself.

She looked down into her tray. There were not many boxes left there. But it was freezing so hard . . . . . .

Another gust of wind came howling down the street, just as she made up her mind not to strike any more matches. Oh,

what did it matter? she asked herself now. She could no longer bear all this suffering.

Quickly, she struck several more matches . . . . .

This time, in the clear trembling flame, a large object began to appear, little by little, and an intense light seemed to shimmer all round it.

"A stove!" she whispered, excitedly. "A beautiful big enamel stove, exactly like the one we had in our house!"

"That's right – so you remember me," she thought it said. "A very good friend of yours, wasn't I? Always warm and glowing. Come a little closer, child. Look at this lovely red charcoal. Closer, closer – I'll send all my warmth out to wrap you up, for goodness knows you need a bit of warmth!"

And the great stove rumbled cheerfully like a friendly old house dog, sent a few cinders rattling out, began to devour a few bits of black charcoal and turn them bright red. In fact it seemed to shake all over, and its lovely carved decorations twinkled in the light.

"It looks as though it's going to blow up!" thought the girl, suddenly worried, for she didn't remember ever seeing the stove quite so bright and red before.

And she was just going to warn the stove not to burn so fast and hot, when the matches in her hand gave a flicker and went out.

Once again the cold night was upon her and she realised that she had been dreaming, that she hadn't really seen the old stove, and she began to cry. Great tears rolled down her

cheeks, and her hunger had become a terrible pain, for she had eaten nothing for two days except some scraps of bread.

Gathering up her strength, she got up, went to the nearest house and knocked at the door. But there was such a noise going on inside that no one heard her.

She went back to her corner and sat down again. Her stock of matches was getting low, but at least there was some comfort in them. She struck another bunch of them .... and suddenly....

A door opened before her. She could see right into a big dining room, full of furniture that shone with polishing. Beautiful lamps were all around, and now she could see a great long table. It was covered with a heavy white cloth, and there was a lot of sparkling silver, but above all, there was food – lots of glorious food just sitting there before her hungry eyes.

On a huge plate there was a great roasted goose, with a golden crackling skin shining with gravy that gave off a delicious odour. It was surrounded by roast potatoes, steaming hot, and she thought how wonderful it would be to break off a wing from the goose, and to crunch a few of the potatoes all dipped in the gravy!

She could smell the delicious food and her mouth was watering. She even stretched out her hand towards it . . .

And her matches went out.

She was in despair. The cold was getting worse and the wind was shrieking. Now she had cramps in her stomach.

For a few minutes she sat there in a stupor, then roused herself, opened another box of matches and took out another little bundle.

They flared up gaily in a good strong flame. Oh, they were beautiful!

Nothing happened at first, then little by little a huge fireplace began to appear, and the little girl held her breath. Now she could see garlands of flowers decorating the white marble of the fireplace, and at last, slowly, majestically, the shape of a great Christmas tree appeared, up, up it went, almost to the ceiling. It was heavy with decorations.

Each branch twinkled gold and silver from glass balls. Some were like mother-of-pearl. Some were brightly coloured. White frost glittered everywhere, and right at the top, shone the Star of Bethlehem. Among the branches of the tree parcels were hidden, full of a thousand and one surprises, waiting to be opened.

And all around there was a delicious pine smell.

Suddenly the tree began to speak in a gentle, sweet voice.

"You know me, don't you, little one? You admired me, didn't you? I was very beautiful, there in your room, but oh, how thirsty I was! All my pine needles were turning yellow. I missed the winds of the forest. My trunk seemed to be roasting – all because I was put there in front of that great roaring fire. And you knew that, didn't you, although you were scarcely more than a baby, and every evening I stood there, you brought water and gave it to my poor parched roots."

"And then you begged your parents to plant me outside in the garden, and they did, thanks to you. And there I grew! And in the summer, you used to play in my shade with your dolls."

44

Oh, yes, she remembered it all very well.

"But what are you doing there, all alone, and wearing those rags?" asked the tree.

"Oh, my dearest Christmas tree," she wept. "Of course I

remember you. When you were growing in the garden I used to think that you bowed your branches to me when I passed, as though you knew me, and I loved that! Do you remember that bed of violets I planted in the moss round your trunk, and the baby squirrel that fell out of your top branches one day and was hurt? I took it to my grandmother and she made it well again."

"She used to come and sit in my shade, too. What has happened to her?" asked the tree.

"Well, after my parents died in a shipwreck, I went to live with my grandmother. She was quite poor, but we lived very happily for a while in a little room, but she became ill and died. That's why I am all alone to-night, Christmas Eve, so cold and hungry. Oh, dear tree, I am so glad to see you! Let me stroke your needles, like I used to do."

But the instant she put out her hand to touch the tree, it faded away into the dark night and she was all alone again.

Quickly she struck more matches and the Christmas tree slowly reappeared, rustling its branches, rattling its decorations, while bright colours flashed and shone.

Her eyes shone like stars and her heart beat loudly. She just sat and watched till the tree faded away again.

And now she had no more matches left.

There was nothing more she could do. She crouched in her corner on the cold stones, in despair. Great sobs shook her. All those dreams of happiness and warmth just made her feel worse.

And then she felt a touch on her shoulder, and the figure of

an old woman appeared before her. With loving blue eyes she
looked at the girl, and a warm, radiant smile lit up her wrinkled
face.

The girl gave a loud cry of joy. "Grandmother! Is it really
you?"

She threw herself forward into the outstretched arms.

"It is really me, little one," said her grandmother, wrapping the frozen feet into her warm woollen shawl. "I have been watching you from the land of the shadows where I now live, and I could no longer bear to see your sufferings. So I asked to be allowed to come and see you. Are you feeling warmer now?"

"Oh, yes, yes! I'm not cold at all any more!"

"My precious, I hoped when I left you that some kind family would take you in and care for you, but no one seemed to notice you, or bother."

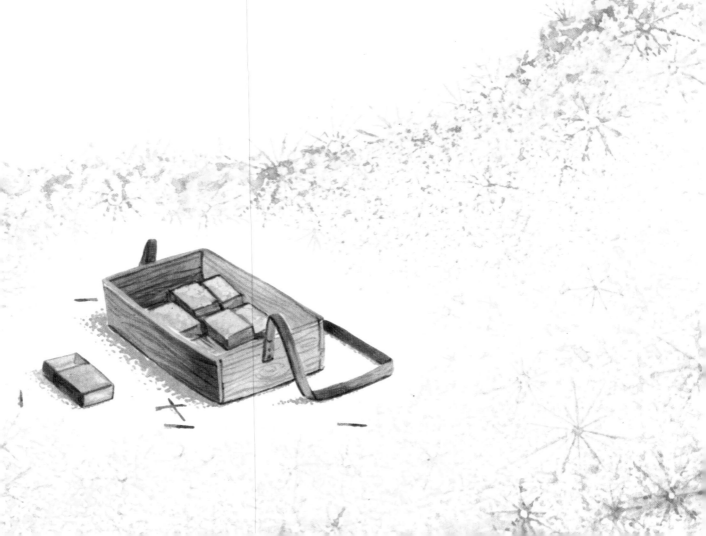

The little girl shook her head and wound her arms round her grandmother's neck. She was smiling now.

"So I am taking you back with me. It is a very different world out there, but you will get used to it and we shall be together again."

And, holding the child in her arms, the grandmother quietly vanished into the night.

Thumbelina

ONE day a kind country woman gave a drink of water to an old beggar, who was really a magician.

In return, the magician gave her a single barley seed, and told her it was a magic seed. She said: "I know you have been wanting a baby for a long time. So, if you will plant this seed in a pot of good soil, and water it every day, you will get a lovely surprise."

The woman was very astonished, but she did as the magician had said, and some time later a great fat flower bud grew out of the soil.

"Oh, it's going to be a peony!" cried the woman, admiring its tightly closed petals. There was nothing extraordinary about it, though. She had plenty of peonies in her garden.

Still, she looked after the plant; bit by bit it opened, and there, sitting in the heart of it, was the tiniest, most beautiful little girl imaginable! And she was no bigger than a thumb!

So the woman called her Thumbelina, and looked after her lovingly. She made her a tiny bed in a large nutshell, and lined it with violet petals.

At night she put the tiny bed back into the peony bloom, but during the day, Thumbelina played on the table where her mother placed a large dish full of water and tiny flowers and grasses. Using a tiny twig as an oar, she could row from side to side of the plate, as though she were crossing a lake.

It was lovely to see her doing this. Her mother thought it was the most charming sight, and never tired of watching little Thumbelina, so happy, so beautiful and contented. She was

always thinking up new ways of pleasing this tiny little girl.

For food, the countrywoman would put a few drops of honey, or milk, in a thimble, and Thumbelina would drink it. And oh, what a pleasure it was to make tiny clothes, and to smooth the long silky hair, while Thumbelina gaily prattled.

This went on and they were very happy. But one night, while Thumbelina slept, a great toad crept through the open window of the room where the peony stood on a table. Being curious, he looked inside the peony and there he saw the lovely, tiny child, peacefully sleeping at the heart of the flower.

"Ha! Ho!" he croaked. "Here's a pretty find! Just what I've been looking for – my eldest son needs a wife!" He picked up the nutshell and in a few leaps he was off, down to the bottom of the garden where there was a stream. This was his kingdom.

Not wishing to waken Thumbelina, he put her on a water-lily leaf which was standing on the stream.

When she awoke the next day, Thumbelina was very frightened to find she was not inside her peony, and began to cry.

"Stop that noise, silly, and meet my eldest son. This fine boy is going to be your husband. Isn't that splendid?"

"Croak, croak," said the younger toad. "When is the wedding to be?"

But he was even uglier than his father. Poor little

Thumbelina began to scream, but no one from the house could hear her.

Oh, what a monster! "Oh, help me, help me!" she called out.

Some fish were swimming underneath the water-lily plant and heard her. Silently they came up to the leaf she was sitting on . . . . .

..... and while the two toads were discussing the wedding and looking the other way, the fish bit through the stem of the water-lily leaf. And immediately the leaf began to sail off down the stream, so fast that the toads could not catch it.

Then Thumbelina laughed for joy because she had escaped from the toads, though she was a tiny bit afraid because the nut-shell boat sailed along the water so quickly.

But at least she was free and the toads couldn't catch her, and she could watch the banks of the stream as they went by.

The trees seemed to bow to her as she passed, and the birds seemed to sing, "Never have we seen anyone so beautiful."

Then a splendid butterfly with great mauve wings began to flutter around her. Suddenly it swooped down, picked up Thumbelina by her belt, and flew off with her, up, up into the air.

"Oh, what fun this is!" cried Thumbelina, clapping her hands with joy.

But a huge water-beetle that had been scurrying around the water had seen this, and thought he would like to have Thumbelina. He snatched her from the butterfly as they passed him, and swooped away, right to the highest branch of the highest tree in the nearby forest.

"Oh! Oh! Please don't eat me, Mr. Water-Beetle!" she screamed.

The water-beetle was not really cruel, and her crying upset him. So he took her down again to the ground, and laid her on a mossy bank. Then he brought nectar from the flowers, a little dew to drink, some tender grass shoots and a few wild strawberries. Thumbelina, who was now very hungry indeed, ate everything and decided the water-beetle was a very friendly person.

But now she was tired, so she made herself a soft bed of moss amongst the roots of a tree, and as the leaves of the tree sheltered her from the rain and the morning dew, she felt very safe there.

In fact it was such a beautiful place that she stayed there.

The summer went on, and she found plenty to eat. New grass shoots were always growing; there were wild strawberries to eat, and ripe bilberries full of juice to drink. A little squirrel gave her a present of an empty acorn cup, and every morning she collected dew in it and was able to have a bath. Whenever she took a bath like this, the tom-tits who lived nearby kept guard, to frighten away any birds of prey.

And so she was not unhappy, neither hungry nor cold, but oh, how she missed her dear mother! All that loving care, all the little songs her mother had sung to her – yes, she did miss these, there in the forest, despite all the kind friends she found there.

But as autumn drew near the nights became cooler. The clothes she had been wearing when the toad carried her off were not warm enough. She had to try and make more clothes for herself, just the way her mother had done.

It was very difficult indeed.

Feathers were too light and she couldn't fasten them together. Leaves were too hard and stiff and they broke apart very easily. She didn't know what to do, and all the time it was getting colder.

She was almost giving up when one day she found a scrap of bright red material hanging on a bush. It was as warm and fine as she could wish. But where could she find some cotton?

Then quite close by where she was sitting, she saw a large spider, spinning its web.

Thumbelina watched in amazement as the spider worked

away from morning till night, spinning long silver threads and weaving a web as beautiful and dainty as the finest place.

"That beautiful thread is just what I need," thought Thumbelina, but the spider seemed so big and busy, she hardly dared ask at first.

But at last she did, and although the spider looked so frightening, she gladly gave Thumbelina some of her thread.

And soon, using a rose thorn as a needle, she had made a warm pretty red skirt for herself.

And not before time, because now the days grew shorter and the wind grew stronger. The flowers and berries on which Thumbelina had fed all disappeared, and underneath her oak tree which now had no leaves, poor Thumbelina shivered.

One morning she found herself covered in fine white ice, and when she stood up, a great gust of wind almost blew her away. She decided she must go and try to find help from somewhere.

As she made her way through a wheat field, she suddenly came upon a tiny door hidden beneath some dried grass. She knocked on the door with all her might.

"I am hungry and alone," she called out. "Please give me something to eat, even if it is only a grain of barley. And I am very cold. Please open the door."

The door did open. And there stood a gentle little field mouse.

"Oh, you poor little girl!" exclaimed the mouse, twitching her tiny nose. "Come in, come in."

"It is warm in here and I have food, because I have collected wood and seeds all through the summer," she went on. "Stay here and get warm. I'll bring you something to eat."

As soon as she had done so, and felt better, Thumbelina got up to leave after thanking the mouse. But the mouse said: "Listen, little girl, you would be doing me a favour if you would stay here with me. The winter is long and I do get a bit bored when I am all alone."

Thumbelina was overjoyed and agreed to stay.

And so the days passed peacefully. She told Mrs. Mouse all about her adventures, and the mouse told her funny stories and made her laugh. And between them they kept the dark little house beautiful, and they had no shortage of food.

And sometimes they were paid a visit by their next door neighbour, Mr. Mole.

One day he arrived wearing a large black hat which had rolled into his underground burrow after someone had lost it. He felt very grand and dressed up.

And as Mr. Mole hardly ever went out of his burrow, he liked to hear Thumbelina talking about life in the world above ground. He thought it was very brave to live on top, instead of underneath, and he was full of wonder.

And every time Thumbelina started to tell her stories, Mr. Mole paraded around wearing his tall black hat and looking fierce.

One day she began to laugh. "Mr. Mole, you are funny!" she cried. "I am sure you could get a job in a circus. With that hat, and baggy trousers, you could be a clown."

Then of course she had to explain to her friends what a circus was. She told them about the clever animals, and the tricks they performed. But when she talked about the clowns and their funny antics, Mr. Mole became vexed and went off home.

Then Mrs. Mouse found an old pipe which some field workers had dropped. She brought it out, filled it with straw, and began to smoke it very fast.

"Pooh! What a dreadful smell!" remarked Thumbelina, and she went on: "Mouse dear, you look just like an old soldier."

"Really, Thumbelina, this is too much!" cried Mrs. Mouse. "You are always complaining and finding fault. Would you rather go and find those old toads and live with them? You can always do that, if you wish."

"Oh, my dear, dear friends, do forgive me!" begged Thumbelina. "I am so sorry. I did not mean to vex you." And she was ashamed of herself.

Then Mr. Mouse and Mr. Mole – who happened to be there that day – hugged Thumbelina, who promised never to grumble again.

But one day, taking a little walk, she found a swallow.

The poor little thing lay on the ground, exhausted with cold and hunger. She knelt down and stroked it and presently it opened one eye. Quickly she ran and found some food for it.

She didn't tell the others about it, but kept it hidden all through the winter, until spring came round, and the swallow wanted to leave.

"Come with me," he invited her. "Climb on my back and I will take you on a wonderful trip to Egypt. You will see the flamingoes beside the river Nile, and I will show you my nest of dry twigs."

Thumbelina sighed. "I would love to come, swallow, but I cannot leave my dear mouse, who cared for me and fed me when I was in great trouble."

"Then good-bye. I will come back next spring to see you," replied the swallow, and flew away.

She was sad after that. Oh, she would have loved to go with him, and life here seemed very dull when the sun began to shine once more across the fields.

And then something else happened. Mr. Mole came round one day and, very formally, asked her to marry him.

"I will come round again to-morrow for your answer," he said, and went.

And Thumbelina began to weep.

"Surely I have not escaped that great ugly toad, only to have to marry Mr. Mole," she wept. "He is too old for me and too serious."

But the mouse said. "I am getting old, child, and who else will care for you? Mr. Mole will make a good husband, for he is kind and a good worker."

So Thumbelina agreed, with a heavy heart, and the wedding was arranged for the month of November, as Mr. Mole wished to gather in as much food as possible, thinking this would please his little bride.

Every day Thumbelina went out into the sunshine, which she would miss so much when she went to live in Mr. Mole's dark burrow under the ground. Sometimes she wept.

She would press her cheek against the satiny petals of the
flowers, play hide and seek with the ladybirds, sip the juice
from the flowers.

Wise Mrs. Mouse could see how unhappy she was, but said
nothing.

Autumn came; the leaves turned yellow and the last harvests
were gathered in from the fields. Busy Mr. Mole rushed here
and there, trying to store up as much winter food as he could.

And then one day, just as he had promised, the swallow
came back to visit Thumbelina.

Oh, how happy she was to see him!

She flung her arms about him, stroked his feathers and kissed him. But he said: "Thumbelina, you look very unhappy. What is the matter?"

She told him that she was soon to marry Mr. Mole.

"Oh, no!" he exclaimed. "That will not do at all! Come with me, Thumbelina. Fly with me to a warm country and let me show you some beautiful sights. You will die if you stay here, and you cannot marry Mr. Mole. Mrs. Mouse understands and she will not be angry."

So Thumbelina told Mrs. Mouse, who said: "The swallow is right. Go with him, child. You will be happy, and perhaps you will think sometimes of your friends in the wheat field."

Thumbelina was delighted and hugged Mrs. Mouse. Then she went to Mr. Mole and very politely told him that she could not marry him, and asked him to forgive her. He listened to her, but though he was annoyed, he wished her a pleasant journey.

"Well, really!" he complained to Mrs. Mouse. "Why should she prefer the sun which hurts the eyes anyway, when she could have the lovely darkness of my house, and all the food I have stored up?"

"Perhaps she is a little too young and gay for such a serious person like yourself," said Mrs. Mouse. "Perhaps she would not have been a good wife for you."

She coaxed him back into a good temper, and they began to plan long games of dominoes when the winter came.

Then off went Thumbelina with the swallow. Perched on his back, with her arms tightly round his neck, they soared into the air and flew on the wind. Sometimes she felt giddy when she looked down and saw the tops of the highest trees below them. Sometimes she had to close her eyes, but she soon opened them again, for she wanted to see everything.

Rivers like silver ribbons. Villages like toy houses with red roofs. Churches looking like little models. People even, looking as tiny as herself.

Oh, what a wonderful world it was! She had been so right to fly away with the swallow. There was nothing like this in the wheat field.

Each evening, when darkness came, the weary swallow

would alight somewhere and they would refresh themselves by some stream, and find something to eat.

For many long days they travelled like this, sometimes joining other groups of birds who were leaving the cold winter behind and flying to the warm suns of Africa. Storks with great wings and long thin feet; great formations of geese and wild ducks with lovely blue wings and green collars.

Thumbelina was delighted with everything she saw.

At last they reached North Africa, and came to rest among

white terraced roofs and the spires of minarets. For the first time Thumbelina tasted the delicious nectar of the great red bougainvillea, while her dear friend the swallow feasted on millet and dry locusts.

Then they went on their way, and one fine morning the majestic river Nile appeared beneath them, and they could see great strange birds called ibises among the reeds on the banks. They had arrived!

They flew down towards a palace with splendid towers, standing in the middle of a great park. And here the swallow set Thumbelina down, near a fine clump of magnolia bushes in full bloom.

"You have arrived, little one," said the swallow. "This is as far as I am taking you. Don't be afraid – great fortune awaits you, and this is where you will find it."

Then before Thumbelina had time to say anything, there was a rustling sound among the leaves. She turned, and saw a great flower bud opening slowly. Its petals were like mother-of-pearl and they opened one by one to show the dark blue heart, where sat a most handsome man, beautifully dressed, who was no bigger than . . . a thumb!

He rose, and bowed gracefully to her.

"You are very welcome to my kingdom, little stranger," he said. "I am the prince of the flowers, and I am at your service."

"For a long time," he went on. "I have been seeking a wife like myself, born like me into the kingdom of flowers."

Thumbelina was so surprised she still could not speak.

"Your friend the swallow told me of you," he said. "And I asked him to go back and bring you. I can see you are just as beautiful as he said. Would you become my wife, Thumbelina?"

Then Thumbelina thought of all her friends and above all, her dear mother. She would never forget any of them, but how wonderful it would be to live here with the Prince, amongst the flowers!

"I shall be very happy," she told him. "And we shall make this park into a resting place for birds, in memory of our friend the swallow."

The Prince smiled, and placed a beautiful gold crown on her head.

Puss In Boots

ONCE upon a time there was a poor miller who died, leaving the mill, a donkey, a cat – and three sons. The eldest son had the mill, the second took the donkey, but the youngest only got the cat. He was not pleased about this.

"It's all right for my brothers," he kept on saying to himself. "They can work together and do very well with the mill and the donkey. But what can I do with a cat? I can eat it, I suppose, and make a fur cap out of its skin. And that's about all."

This went on and on, till one day the cat said:

"Master, why don't you stop moaning? Now, if you will give me a bag, and provide me with some boots so that I can walk through the rough parts of the forest in comfort, I will prove to you that you are not so badly off as you think!"

His master nearly fell over with shock when he heard this. Goodness, his cat could talk! Never had he come across such a thing! Then he began to wonder what the cat could possibly do with a sack and a pair of boots.

"Just leave that to me," said the cat, and went off to town with the money his master gave him. Here he bought a sack, a smart pair of high leather boots and also a very elegant suit. He looked very fine dressed in these things.

Then he filled the sack with carrots and lettuces, flung it over his shoulder, and went off to a very fine warren in the forest, where a lot of large, plump rabbits lived.

In the warren, he opened his sack and put it on the ground, then lay down beside it and stretched himself out, pretending to be dead so as not to frighten the rabbits who would soon come along when they smelled the carrots and lettuces, their favourite foods.

He didn't have long to wait. A large rabbit soon arrived and sniffed around. After a while he crept into the sack and began to nibble away ... then ... wham! The cat leapt at him, and killed him with one blow.

This happened several more times, till at last the cat had a sackful of fine rabbits. Then he closed the sack, flung it over his shoulder and went off – to the king's palace!

The servants at the palace were very surprised to see a cat, smartly dressed, wearing boots and able to talk in human language. So polite, too, as he asked to see the king.

Of course the king did not usually have cats visiting him, but this one was so unusual that they could not refuse, and took him into the audience chamber.

"What a strange thing – a cat visiting the king," said the knights and lords to each other, and they watched him curiously as he strutted along. But he was so dignified that no one tried to make fun of him. Not a smile was seen, not a laugh was heard.

The cat walked up to the king and bowed deeply. "Sire," he said. "I have brought you some fine rabbits which my master, the Marquis of Carabas, would like you to accept."

He had invented this fine title, which sounded much better than the name of the poor miller's son.

The king was delighted with the gift, and said so. "Please tell your master I am very pleased, and thank him for me," he said.

The cat made another fine bow and left, knowing he would soon be back at this palace.

Some time later he went to the woods again, and this time he caught some fine partridges. Again he took them to the king and said they were a present from his master.

The old king was again delighted. He called the cat Mr. Puss-in-Boots and ordered food and drink to be brought for him. While the cat was eating and drinking, he told him to be sure to thank his master, the kind Marquis of Carabas.

The cat said he would certainly not forget, and went on making his plans.

During the next two or three months he brought many more gifts to the king. It was always food, for it was well known that the king liked eating. So fine hares, plump quails, brightly coloured pheasants, wild ducks and woodcocks were laid before the king, and Puss-in-Boots always said his master had caught them, out hunting in his woods.

The king had never heard of the Marquis of Carabas, and began asking questions about him, and sending his very best wishes to this kind gentleman.

By now of course, everyone in the palace was curious about all these visits and about the Marquis of Carabas, whom no one knew.

They gossiped among themselves, and made all kinds of guesses.

So the cat now decided to put a stop to all this mystery and talk, and began looking around for a chance to introduce his master to the king, which of course was what he had intended all the time. And soon, an opportunity came. One day, leaving the palace, he almost bumped into an old washer-woman who was just bringing some clean linen.

She was very annoyed with him.

"Look where you're going, Master Puss-in-Boots!" she

snapped. "You nearly made me drop the lace tablecloth which the king and the princess will be using for their picnic to-morrow."

Immediately, Puss-in-Boots saw his chance.

"I do beg your pardon," he said, politely. "And where are the king and the princess going for their picnic to-morrow?"

But she pushed him away and went off. He did not pester her, but went off into the forest and caught a large rabbit, which he took back to the palace and gave to one of the servants.

"I thought you might like this for your supper," said Puss-in-Boots.

The servant was very surprised and pleased, and thought what a friendly sort of cat Puss-in-Boots was. He took the rabbit and thanked Puss-in-Boots, who began chatting away, asking about the king and the princess . . . . .

And in no time at all he had found out where the royal party would be going for their picnic to-morrow. He also learned which road they would be taking, and that they would be driving very close to the river.

This was it! He rushed home to his master. "Now listen to me, Master. If you will do exactly as I say, your fortune is made!"

He explained what his master had to do.

"It is perfectly easy. All you have to do is take a swim in the river at a certain place which I am going to show you. That's all. Just leave the rest to me."

The young man had no idea what it was all about, but he trusted his clever cat, took off his clothes and went into the water.

Here he just swam about in a circle, waiting for something to happen and watching the cat, who marched up and down and kept looking away across the fields, as though he were expecting to see someone.

And at last, they did see someone. Away in the distance the royal coach appeared – a beautiful coach , drawn by four fine prancing horses.

And now the cat gathered up all his master's poor ragged clothes and hid them under a large stone. Then, as the coach came nearer, he began waving his arms and shouting at the top of his voice.

"Help! Help! The Marquis of Carabas is here drowning! Help! Help!"

The king heard these cries, stopped the horses and jumped out of the coach. And of course, he recognised the cat who had brought him all those splendid gifts of food from his master.

He ordered his servants to go to the rescue, and while they did so, the cat told him that while his master was bathing, thieves had stolen all his clothes. The king became very angry at this, and immediately sent a servant back to the palace to bring back some clothes for the marquis. And when the young man finally stood there, dressed in the king's own clothes, looking very proud and handsome, everyone agreed that he was a fine looking young man.

The princess smiled at him, too, and found him very much to her liking.

The king told the Marquis of Carabas that he was delighted to meet him, and invited him into the royal coach. He suggested he might like to come along and share their picnic.

So far the cat's plans were working out, but he hadn't finished yet.

He left them, and ran on ahead. Soon, he saw some labourers ploughing a field. He went up to them and said commandingly:

"Good people, the king is coming this way. You must tell him that all these lands belong to the Marquis of Carabas. If you don't you will all be killed."

They were astonished, but agreed to do this. And when the royal coach arrived, the king did ask, and they all replied:

"Sire, these lands belong to the Marquis of Carabas."

Meanwhile the cat hurried on ahead, repeated the same threat to more field workers getting in the harvest. And so it went for a long distance, and everywhere the royal coach passed, the king got the same answer, till he began to think that the Marquis of Carabas was not only a very charming young man, but a very wealthy one, too. And he could see that his daughter was falling in love with the marquis, and this pleased him, too.

Meanwhile, Puss-in-Boots had now arrived at a great castle.

He learned from a gardener that the castle was owned by a great ogre, who was immensely rich, powerful and evil, who owned all the land hereabouts for miles.

Puss-in-Boots asked if he might speak to this great person, and as the ogre happened that day to be all alone, he agreed to see his unexpected visitor.

So the cat was shown in, made his usual deep bow, and began to pay the ogre a lot of flattering compliments.

This surprised the ogre very much, but presently he ordered food and drink to be brought in.

The cat chattered on, talking of this and that, when suddenly he said:

"Sir, I have been told that you have the power of changing yourself into any kind of animal, for example a lion or even an elephant. Is this true? I have never heard of such a thing before. Surely someone has been trying to pull my leg?"

Now the ogre became very angry indeed. He jumped up straight, and the cat now saw that he was very, very large indeed. He gave a loud roar, and Puss-in-Boots began to tremble.

But he had been counting on this creature's vanity, and he saw that his trick was going to work.

"Of course I can change myself!" shouted the ogre, full of rage and red in the face. "Are you trying to annoy me? Then I will prove it to you. Just watch – I will now change myself into a lion, before your very eyes. Grrr .... grrr .... "

And in less time than it takes to tell, the ogre had changed into a lion, fierce and terrifying, with shining red eyes, a thick bristling mane, sharp claws and powerful muscles.

The cat was absolutely terrified. He turned and fled up to the top of a cupboard, and didn't dare to come down until the ogre had changed back into his own shape.

"Oh, that was marvellous!" said the cat. "Oh, what a fright you gave me! Oh, what a wonderful lion you were! Oh, what a clever person you are!"

The ogre waved his hand.

"That's nothing," he said. "I do it all the time just for fun. It amuses me when I've nothing else to do."

"You were a very big lion." said the cat. "Is it very hard to do it?"

"Not at all. I've just told you."

"But do you only change into large animals? Can you do it with small animals, too? Could you change into a rat, for instance, or a mouse?"

"You name it, I can change into it," said the ogre. He was beginning to be bored with the cat.

"A mouse, did you say?" he went on, and in the blink of an eyelid, he had changed into a tiny mouse which ran swiftly across the floor.

Then the cat, who had planned exactly this, leapt on to the mouse and killed him instantly. Then he ate him.

And now the castle had no master. Puss-in-Boots immediately called all the servants, told them that the ogre had left suddenly, forever, and their new master was called the Marquis of Carabas. All the servants cheered.

He also said that the marquis would be arriving very soon, bringing with him a large party of very important personages. And by the time they arrived, he said, this castle must be ready to greet them properly, with a fine banquet prepared, and everything bright and shining.

The servants were very pleased to hear this, for the ogre had been very careless and dirty, and the castle was very neglected.

Right away they all set to work. The cooks and the kitchen staff began planning their very best dishes, with the finest food and tastiest sauces and most beautiful decorations. They were all determined to do their best for their new master and his guests.

And while the kitchens buzzed with activity, the footmen, the valets, the chamber maids and other servants bustled around, cleaning up the dining room, the great drawing rooms and all the bedrooms.

There was a lot to do, but it must be done. For who would ever believe that the elegant Marquis of Carabas lived in such a neglected place?

So everything was in an uproar, but the work went on. Puss-in-Boots walked around all the time, giving orders and acting like a high-born noble.

But soon things began to look different. Great vases of fresh flowers were stood around everywhere. Tables were laid in the dining hall, with beautiful white cloths, dishes and cutlery of solid gold and silver. And in the meantime, the work in the kitchens went on, and the great feast was almost ready.

And now the royal coach could be seen nearing the castle. The king was astonished at all the magnificence, and stared out of his window, admiring everything.

Then Puss-in-Boots ran up to the royal coach and cried loudly: "Your Majesty! Welcome to the home of the Marquis of Carabas! Won't you do us the honour of coming inside, and eating with us?"

And he swept off his plumed hat and bowed deeply to the king.

"Thank you very much," replied the king, very impressed with all the grandeur, the extent of the lands, the beauty of the gardens, and the many servants he could see hurrying about.

So, with the princess on one side of him, and the Marquis of Carabas on the other, the king entered the castle. Behind him came all the fine people, nobles and their ladies, who had set out with him that morning just for a picnic. They were all just as surprised as the king.

Inside the castle all the doors had been flung wide open. Puss-in-Boots led them from room to room, along corridors full of sunshine from bright long windows. And at last they reached the dining hall, where the tables were laid, and the gold and silver and crystal glass sparkled in the rays of the sun.

"Sir," said the king to the Marquis. "I never realised I lived so close to such a remarkable man as yourself."

"Your Majesty does me great honour," replied the Marquis, looking at his clever cat.

All the tables had been laid down the room, but one smaller

table stood alone at the top, and here Puss-in-Boots led the king, the princess and his master.

The rest of the party were seated at the other tables, with servants to wait on them. But Puss-in-Boots himself waited on the top table.

The feasting began, and such a feast it was! Such roasts and pies and turkeys and chickens! Such delicious vegetables grown in the castle gardens! Such fine wines and exquisite fruits!

"Never," said the king. "Have I eaten such wonderful food or seen such splendid tables! Truly, my dear Marquis, you are a most gracious host."

And he smiled as he watched his daughter the princess chatting to the Marquis, laughing at his jokes, eating a slice of peach which he offered to her on a fork.

As their king was looking so happy, the nobles and ladies were also enjoying themselves, and soon the great fine hall was full of laughter and gaiety. They also noticed how gay the lovely young princess was and how she seemed to like the handsome young marquis, and began to whisper between themselves if perhaps there might soon be a royal wedding? They hoped so, for there was nothing like a royal wedding for show and pomp and lots of splendid new clothes.

And in fact the king was thinking almost the same thing. This fine young man, he thought, so handsome, and well-mannered, and so rich – what a husband he would be for the princess! What a son-in-law for the king!

He leaned across and whispered to the two young people. The princess blushed. The Marquis took her hand and looked very proud.

Then the king stood up and everyone became silent.

"My dear friends," he said. "You will all be very happy to know that I have consented to a marriage between our beloved princess and our host, the Marquis of Carabas!"

They all began to cheer.

And while they cheered, and raised their glasses to the

happy couple, the Marquis of Carabas wondered if he were dreaming.

He knew he was really only the son of a poor miller, and not a marquis. Yet suddenly he found himself very rich, and engaged to marry a beautiful young princess . . . .

Then he looked at his cat, Puss-in-Boots, and knew he was very lucky indeed to have such a magical cat, who had brought about all these marvels.

"Dear Puss-in-Boots, I am grateful to you. I shall always love you and you shall have anything you wish," thought the Marquis. "And I shall do my best to be a good husband to the princess, and in time a real marquis."

The cat winked at him, and went on listening to the king.

SNOW

A very kind and beautiful queen was one day sitting by her window, sewing, when she pricked her finger, and a large drop of blood appeared.

"Ah," she sighed. "How I would like to have a little daughter with lips as red as this blood; skin as white as the snow outside, and hair as black as the ebony wood of my chair! How happy I would be!"

Some time later her wish came true, and she had the most beautiful little baby. Her parents were overjoyed, and called her Snow White.

WHITE

Just as the queen had wished, the little princess had snowy white skin, rich black hair and a lovely mouth with lips of bright red.

But alas! Not long after she was born, the queen died.

The king was very unhappy, but presently he married again, a very beautiful woman who was very jealous. And because the baby princess was so lovely, the new queen sent her away from the court, to be kept in the furthest part of the castle and to be cared for by the servants.

Although she no longer saw her father, the princess was quite happy. But then one day the king also died, and there was only the queen left.

Now the queen had a magic mirror, which had been given to her by her godmother, who was a magician. And every morning the queen asked the mirror the same question.

"Tell me, mirror, who is the most beautiful person in this kingdom?"

And always the mirror gave the same reply. "Your Majesty, you are the most beautiful person in the kingdom."

And so fifteen years passed. The queen led a very fine life, while the little princess never even saw the court. But she was happy, and everyone loved her.

Then one morning when the queen asked the mirror her usual question, it replied: "Indeed your Majesty is very beautiful, but the princess Snow White is now more beautiful than you are."

The mirror, of course, could never tell a lie.

But when she heard this, the queen was very angry, and she sent for one of her woodsmen. She said to him, very angrily:

"John, I order you to take the princess Snow White out to the very heart of the forest. There you will kill her, and as proof that you have obeyed me, you will bring me back her heart."

The woodsman was horrified. "Oh, no, no!" he cried.

"Silence! You will do as I say! And if you disobey me, or try to deceive me, you will spend the rest of your life in prison."

The woodsman did not want to spend the rest of his life in prison, so that evening, although he felt very unhappy, he went for the princess Snow White, and pretending they were going to pick mushrooms, he led her far, far away, right into the middle of the great forest.

It was a very special treat for Snow White to be taken out

99

like this, and at first she enjoyed it, picking mushrooms and flowers, chattering away to the woodsman. But they were going further and further away from the castle, deeper and deeper into the forest.

At last, as it was becoming dark, the woodsman stopped, and drew out his knife.

"What are you doing?" asked Snow White. "Why have you drawn your knife?"

"Princess," said the man. "I have to tell you that your stepmother the Queen ordered me to bring you here and kill you. Forgive me, Princess. I cannot do it, of course, but go – go – go now – anywhere – far away where she can't find you – or sure enough we shall both die."

Then he walked quickly away from her, caught a deer and removed its heart, then went back to the castle. He did not look at Snow White again, and full of fear, she ran as fast as she could.

She had no idea where to go, and it was getting darker all the time. She was already very tired, and this was the first time she had been in the forest. It was a new world to her, and everything was frightening.

Wings beat around her as she ran. Great twisted roots of trees caught her feet and time after time she fell. Once a pair of large golden eyes stared at her from the undergrowth, and she thought they belonged to a demon. A long growth of ivy brushed her and it seemed to be a snake. And she was running in all directions.

For a long time this went on, until suddenly she came upon a clearing covered with grass, and here she rested. But as her eyes became used to the darkness, she saw that this was the spot where the woodsman had left her. She had been going round and round in circles.

"I must find a way!" she told herself. "The queen is clever, and if she suspects the woodsman she will start a search and find me. She will not let me escape a second time."

What she did not know was that all around her, hidden

among the bushes and the trees, a whole lot of forest folk had
been watching her curiously.

"I know her," said an old rabbit, twitching his ears. "She is
the young princess from the castle. I have seen her many times
when I have been eating grass near the tower where she lives."

"A real princess!" exclaimed a young fawn. "So what is she

doing here in the forest, in the middle of the night, running round in circles? We must take her back to the castle, or she will die."

"Hoo-hoo – yes," said an old owl, blinking his great golden eyes. "And I will guide her, for I can see in the dark. Wake her up – she's gone to sleep."

"Not so fast," replied the rabbit. "Late this evening I was near a nut tree, and I heard a woodsman telling his friend that the evil queen had ordered him to take Snow White into the forest and kill her, but he couldn't do it. What we must do is find a safe hiding place for her, where the queen will never find her."

"Let us all think," said the owl, solemnly.

They all thought. Suddenly the fawn exclaimed: "I know! What about the house of the seven dwarfs? My mother took me there and they hid me when hunters were all over the place. It is a long way off, on the other side of the mountain. No one will ever find the princess there!"

"A very good idea," said the owl. "The dwarfs are very kind hearted. They will let this lovely young princess stay with them. Now, who will lead her to where they live?"

They talked about this for a while. But a robin redbreast begged to be allowed to take Snow White.

"She has always been kind to us," he said. "In the winter, when there are no berries, she always put out food for us, every day."

So it was agreed that the robin should guide Snow White.

Then the robin flew down to Snow White and gently fluttered his wing against her cheek, and presently she opened her eyes, stretched her arms, and looked around her. The robin hopped on to a branch and began to sing loudly.

In spite of all her trouble, the princess had to smile.

"Why, I know you!" she cried. "You are the cheeky little bird who used to come right up to my table for crumbs. Are you trying to tell me something?"

He sang some more notes, then flew a little way, perched on another branch, sang again and then came back. He did this several times and at last the princess understood.

"You want me to come with you? Is that it? You are going to show me the way to go? Oh, yes, I will come – but don't fly too fast, will you?"

"Trrr-trrr-trrr," sang the bird, and began flying just ahead of Snow White.

Snow White knew the birds loved her, as she loved them. She could even understand some of their language. So she was happy to follow the robin.

They went a long way, and now it was full daylight.

And Snow White began to understand that a lot of other little folk were all trying to help her. For instance, a handful of freshly gathered nuts suddenly fell at her feet, and she ate them gratefully. The footprints of a rabbit kept appearing before her to show her an easy path to walk.

And all the time the robin went ahead of her, and his sweet song cheered her up.

Then, after a long time, Snow White suddenly saw a thin trickle of smoke rising from the chimney of the strangest little house she had ever seen.

And the robin redbreast flew on to the roof, stopped there, and sang as loudly as he could. "I understand!" said Snow White. "This is where you want me to stay."

When she knocked at the door there was no reply, so she opened it and walked in. She was surprised to find herself in a very small room, full of very small furniture, but with everything in a terrible state of untidiness.

A long low table was laid with seven places, and at each place there was a bowl, with a small glass standing beside it. And over the fire, hanging from a hook, there was a pot, simmering away and giving the most delicious smell.

Snow white realised she was very hungry.

"I wonder if the people who live here would be very angry if I ate a little of their dinner?" she asked herself. "I am sure they are kind people."

So she helped herself from the pot, then she went up some very steep stairs and found seven little beds in a room. She lay down on one of them, stretched herself out, and immediately went to sleep. On and on she slept. She was very tired.

Had she been awake, she would have heard a gay

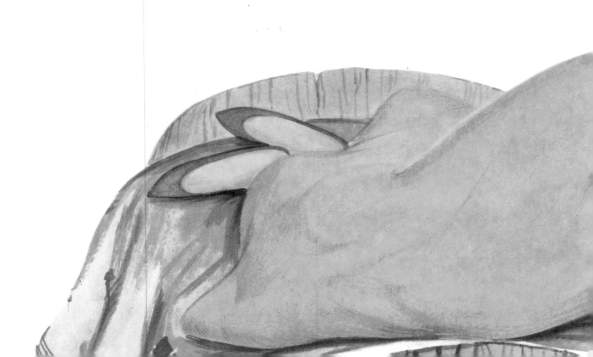

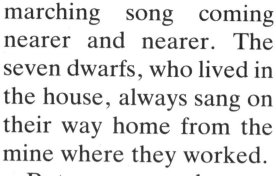

marching song coming nearer and nearer. The seven dwarfs, who lived in the house, always sang on their way home from the mine where they worked.

But as soon as they entered the house, one of them cried out: "Who has been eating out of my bowl, and pushed my chair here?"

They all stared. "Well, really!" they all said together. After all, they hadn't been expecting visitors.

"Oh, yes, someone has been at the cooking pot," said another one. "And they've gone upstairs."

"We'll all go up together and see who it is," they all said, feeling a little bit frightened.

Up they went in a bunch, pushing each other a bit. Very carefully they opened the bedroom door . . . and the smallest one cried out: "She's here!"

They rushed forward to waken her, but stopped, suddenly.

"Oh, isn't she beautiful!" they gasped.

Yes, she was beautiful, a lovely young girl, with long black hair flowing over her shoulders, a pretty face and rosy cheeks. But even in her sleep, she kept sobbing.

"She seems very unhappy," the dwarfs said to each other.

Just then Snow White awoke and saw seven faces staring at her. But they looked kind faces. They even smiled at her. And when they spoke to her gently, she began telling them why she was here. They were all very shocked indeed.

"Oh, that wicked queen!" said one.

"She must never find you again!"

"Poor child, you can stay here, and from now on you will be happy."

"Do you think you would like it here? It is very lonely, but no one will know and the wicked queen will never find you."

Then Snow White clapped her hands and cried out with joy. "Oh, dear, dear dwarfs, how good you are! I would love to stay here with you, and see – I will look after you all, and keep your house nice and clean!"

And they all went downstairs, and after supper the dwarfs brought out their instruments and played and sang and danced for Snow White.

It was one of the best evenings Snow White had ever had.

She knew she was going to be very happy, and thought how lucky she was, and how kind and gentle all her new friends were.

And so she settled down in the tiny home, away from the wickedness of the queen, protected by the great forest which grew all around.

Every morning the dwarfs set off for the diamond mine underneath the mountain, where they worked, with their pickaxes over their shoulders. Before they left, they always gave her the same advice.

"Do not speak to any strangers, and don't let anyone into the house."

"Don't go any further than the clearing or you will get lost again in the forest."

"And don't work too hard, dear child."

She assured them all, waved them off, then set to work to look after the house. She was a very good housekeeper. The stove had never been so well polished, or the lamps burned so brightly, or the furniture so gleaming. She even looked after their clothes, and the dwarfs became very proud of how they looked.

Each evening when they came home, a tasty meal was ready for them.

During the day she had the birds for company. Robins, warblers, finches came around, waiting for crumbs, trying to see who could sing the loudest. The robin who had guided her here usually perched on her shoulder, and came into the house when she was baking cakes, to watch her.

And Snow White would sing back to them, and then all the forest animals listened, and thought how lovely her voice was.

But of course she sometimes missed her dear old nurse, who had cared for her since she was a baby. The dwarfs realised this, so every Sunday evening they made an extra special concert for her.

She knew they were trying very hard to make her happy, and she loved every one of them. She taught them a few old songs they didn't know, and sometimes danced with them.

All this time, the queen was very happy in her castle, quite certain that now there was no one more beautiful than she was. But one day she took it into her head to ask the mirror the old question. "Mirror, who is the most beautiful person?"

She couldn't believe it when the mirror replied: "Your Majesty, the princess Snow White, who is hidden away in the house of the seven dwarfs, is more beautiful than you."

She flew into a rage, had the woodsman arrested and thrown into prison, and then planned her revenge.

She found a splendid apple and put some strong poison into it, then, disguised as a very old woman dressed in rags, she went off alone, and at last she found the house of the seven dwarfs. She knocked at the door, and at first Snow White would not open it. But then the queen begged:

"I am dying of thirst, dear child. It is so hot. I am old and fainting. Won't you please give me a drink of water?"

And she begged again. "Please, have pity on me."

When Snow White heard this, she could no longer refuse. She opened the door, took the poor old woman inside and gave her a chair, then brought her a glass of clear cold water with a sprig of fresh mint in it.

"Oh, delicious," croaked the old woman. "I feel better now. Take this beautiful apple, child. It is all I have to give you."

Snow White took the apple and bit into it. No sooner was a piece in her mouth than a terrible pain seized her and she fell down, unconscious.

"Ha, ha!" laughed the wicked queen. "Now I am once more the most beautiful person in the kingdom!" And she hurried off.

From the window, the robin redbreast had seen everything, but could not warn Snow White.

114

Now he flew off to the diamond mine, and gave such terrible cries that the dwarfs realised something terrible had happened. They rushed home and found Snow White lying on the floor.

Full of sadness, they made a beautiful coffin of crystal glass for her, and laid her in a small clearing, which they planted with flowers and visited every day.

A long time went by, then one day a young prince who was hunting in the forest, arrived at the clearing and saw the glass coffin.

"Why are you all crying?" he asked the seven dwarfs, who were there. "Is it because of this beautiful girl sealed up in this coffin?"

"Yes, sir. She was our dear Snow White," they replied.

Just at that moment something startled the prince's horse. He jumped back and one foot crashed into the coffin and broke it. The sudden jerk caused the piece of apple which was still in Snow White's mouth to fall out . . . and she opened her eyes and looked around.

Then the prince lifted her on to his white horse and carried her to his kingdom, followed by the seven dwarfs.

They were married soon after, and when the wicked queen heard of this, she fell into a terrible fit of rage, and soon afterwards she died.

HEIDI

ONE bright summer afternoon, a pretty little girl was climbing a path into the Swiss Alps. With her was a young woman wearing an embroidered pinafore in the Swiss style.

The little girl played about, picking flowers here and there – field anemones, scented jacinths, sometimes eating a few ripe blackberries or bilberries. Suddenly she turned and looked backwards, down the mountain, and there lying below her, looking very small, she could see the small town they had left a few hours earlier.

"Look, Aunt Detty!" she cried. "I can see our house! It looks just like a musical box. I can recognise it by the green shutters."

Aunt Detty smiled sadly, but did not reply. They went on. Presently they arrived in a small village, bright with balconies full of red geraniums. A stout village woman who was watering her front garden called out to them.

"Hullo, Detty! What good wind blows you this way? And isn't this little Heidi? Good heavens, child, how you've grown. And where are you going?"

"I'm taking Heidi to her grandfather. I've been looking after her for four years now, since her parents died. But now I have to earn some money, so I've got a job in Germany, and I can't take her there."

The woman looked serious, and began to whisper into her ear. Heidi heard one or two words, like "mean ... bad-tempered ... never goes to church ... plays cards all by himself ..." And she knew they were talking about her grandfather.

Then the woman patted Heidi's cheek and gave her a juicy peach. They went on.

Heidi didn't know her grandfather, and what she had just heard sounded terrible. But she bit her lip, and decided she just had to make the best of it, seeing that Aunt Detty had to leave her.

They turned out of the village and began to climb another steep path leading upwards through masses of tall fir trees. She watched a little red squirrel, and forgot to feel unhappy. Then suddenly a small white shape bounded on to the path with a clatter of little hooves, and a baby goat stared at her with shining eyes.

A moment later a young boy appeared, driving before him a small herd of goats.

"I'm sorry," he said. "That's Loretta." He stroked the little goat's head. "She's only a baby and she's disobedient. She's always going off and eating the leaves off the peach trees. I am Peter, the goatherd," he said.

"And I am Heidi and I'm going to live with my grandfather who lives in these mountains," replied Heidi. "Do you know him?"

Peter nodded. "Oh, yes. I look after his goats as well as my own, and take them up to the high meadows every morning to feed."

"Hurry now, Heidi," said Aunt Detty, coming up to them. "I can see your grandfather's chalet. And don't forget I have to come back down here before it gets dark."

"But auntie, this boy knows grandfather. He looks after his goats," said Heidi, and she smiled at Peter as they went past him.

At last they could see a pleasant little chalet made of pine wood. Heidi thought it looked lovely, built there in a clearing amongst the dark fir trees.

And then she saw the silent old man standing on the doorstep.

Aunt Detty seemed very embarrassed and began to explain.

"Uncle, this is your granddaughter Heidi. You will have to look after her from now on while I go to Germany to work and earn some money. I don't know how long I'll be away. I'll come back for her when I can."

The old man said nothing, but his face grew angry. Then he suddenly growled: "I never heard of such cheek! Be off out of my sight, both of you!"

But Aunt Detty, very red in the face, set down her niece's suitcase, gave her a great big hug, then turned and hurried off without a word.

Heidi felt terribly alone and afraid, then. She hung her head. But then the unpleasant old man suddenly sat down on his seat, lit his pipe and began to smoke. All the time he stared at her.

Suddenly he said: "So you're Heidi, and I'm stuck with you. Hm, hm. Well, what do you want to do?"

"Please may I see inside your house, Grandfather?" she whispered.

"Certainly. Come in." He got up and opened the door.

Inside there was a room full of shining old furniture, with little windows set into thick walls, opening on to the most beautiful view in the world. There was an alcove with the old man's bed in it.

"I suppose you want something to eat," he growled, and pointed to the table, where delicious-smelling cooked cheese

was ready. "Sit down, then," he said.

And he brought a low table, laid her place on it, and gave her a little stool to sit on. It was a milkmaid's stool, he told her.

Heidi was beginning to feel a little happier now, and after the meal he took her up a narrow rough staircase to a tiny attic, which had one small round window, and a floor that creaked and groaned under her feet.

"Oh, grandfather, do I sleep here?" she cried. "It's lovely! Oh, I'm going to be happy here, I know!"

And she flung her arms about him and kissed him.

He seemed a little pleased at this, and said: "Well, you'd better get off to bed, I suppose."

She was asleep in only a few minutes.

The next morning she was awakened by a loud whistling. She ran to the window and there below was Peter, drawing water from the well for her to wash herself. She dressed and ran outside. The water was terribly cold, but soon she was glowing all over and her cheeks were like rosy apples.

"Oh, grandfather, I slept like a log!" she cried, when she went indoors for breakfast.

"Splendid. So let's have breakfast, and afterwards if you like you can take the goats with Peter up the mountain."

She ate a good breakfast and washed up the dishes, and her grandfather gave her a basket with food in it.

"You take this and go on ahead," he said. "I'll follow you later. And Peter, take good care of Heidi."

Heidi was beginning to think her grandfather was not so mean and bad-tempered, after all.

Peter whistled to the goats, and off they went. It was a glorious morning, and already bees were humming around, heavy with pollen. The goats browsed on mulberry leaves as they climbed upwards, and Heidi filled her apron with wild flowers. Peter found a stick and trimmed it for Heidi.

Soon they arrived at an open meadow, full of rich grass, and here they stopped to rest. The goats played around, looking for the juiciest grass, sometimes bumping into Heidi and knocking her down, till she rolled about and screamed with laughter.

She was as happy as she had ever been since her parents died, as she played there on the mountain with the goats. Beautiful scenery surrounded her. Wild flowers nodded at her and the air was pure and fresh and clean.

And coming up the slopes she could see her grandfather. She waved and called out to him.

And just at that moment, two enormous birds flew slowly above them, calling out in loud voices.

"Oh, what are they?" cried Heidi, and her grandfather, who just arrived, said:

"They are eagles. They often fly around here, but no one knows where their nest is. They are strong birds, and can carry off young sheep, or baby goats, in their great claws."

Heidi shivered as she watched them. But then her grandfather handed her a glass of warm milk and she drank it thirstily, and ate smoked ham and sharp cheese on thick slices of country bread.

Then the two children stretched themselves out on the grass, while the old man took a little walk round.

"Peter, I think I am very happy," said Heidi. "I think I shall like living here."

"I am happy, too," said the boy. "I feel very bored sometimes because I am alone a great deal, but now that you are here I don't feel lonely any more."

The time passed quickly. Peter showed to Heidi how to make whistles out of reeds; how to discover birds' nests, and where to find wild strawberries. He asked her if she would come to the village to visit his grandmother, and she promised she would.

And at last the happy day ended, and it was time to go home.

As the days went on her grandfather became very kind to her. He began to make a bedroom suite just for Heidi, and when it was finished it looked just right in her attic.

Heidi clapped her hands when she saw it. "Oh, grandfather, it is lovely!" she cried. "How clever you are!"

"Yes, well, you need something to put your things in," he said. But he was very pleased that she was happy.

Yes, they were happy days, and now Heidi went out regularly with Peter, to take the goats up the mountain. Long golden days they were, and when the old man came up after them, he would take Heidi by the hand and teach her about the woods; the names of the trees and bushes; the small animals and the birds. Often she was so tired when they arrived home that she fell asleep at supper, and her grandfather would have to carry her up to bed.

But then the days became shorter and colder and it began to snow. Now they could not go up the mountain, but Heidi learned how to paint flowers on the wooden bowls that her grandfather made in his workshop and sold in the village.

So she kept busy, though she did not see Peter now, for the snow was too heavy for him to climb up to the chalet, and the goats were kept in a shed.

Not until the snow stopped falling did Peter come to visit them, and then the old man said, "Well, Peter, it's time for you to go to school again, isn't it?"

Peter made a long face. He detested school, and never liked his lessons.

"Why do I have to go to school?" he asked. "I would rather stay home and look after my goats."

"But goats are not good teachers. You will only grow up into a donkey with them," replied the old man.

Peter blushed, and promised he would try harder at school.

Then he reminded Heidi that his grandmother was still waiting to meet her.

So a few days later her grandfather wrapped her up in a thick overcoat, perched her behind him on his sledge, and after a wild journey down the mountain they stopped in a great flurry of snow outside a neat little house in the village, where Peter's grandmother lived.

She was a very kind lady, and invited them in and gave them hot tea and cakes.

And after she had listened to Heidi for a while and watched her happy laughing face, she decided that the old man who lived up in the mountains was perhaps not so bad as people said he was.

Another happy summer came and passed. Then another winter. And one day, without any warning, the door opened and Aunt Detty walked in.

She looked very brisk and smart in new city clothes, and told them right away that she had come to fetch Heidi and take her back.

The old man was so surprised that he dropped a plate, but Aunt Detty didn't give him a chance to speak.

"She will live with a very rich family. They also have a little girl called Claire, but she is an invalid. Heidi will be a playmate for her and they will have lessons together. It is time Heidi began to learn reading and writing. I know you haven't bothered to send her to school, Uncle. Well, I mean to see that she has some education."

Suddenly, Heidi felt very unhappy, but there was nothing she or her grandfather could do. Aunt Detty made her pack her clothes there and then, and off they went.

It was a very long journey in a train, but a fine carriage met them at the station and drove them to a splendid house. Heidi's new friend Claire was waiting for her, but alas, she had to lie flat in a long chair. Heidi felt very sorry for her and kissed her warmly.

She told herself that she must try and be a good friend to

poor Claire, who was so weak.

Soon they all settled down comfortably and the whole family were very kind to Heidi. She grew to love Claire and they did become good friends, and had their lessons together.

But living in a town did not suit Heidi. She missed the mountains and the good air; her grandfather and the cosy little chalet; Peter and all the goats. She tried very hard but she fretted a lot, and soon she too became a sick little girl.

The doctor was called in, and said there was only one thing to do ... Heidi must go back to her mountains and her grandfather.

This did not please Aunt Detty, but Heidi was overjoyed and clapped her hands.

So back they went, and she could hardly keep still in her excitement. And at last she arrived, and oh! how wonderful it was to be home, to see her grandfather and Peter and the goats and the mountains again. How happy she was! She was almost better after only a few days.

But she did not forget her friend Claire. Her grandfather, who had also been unhappy while she was away, said she could invite Claire to spend a holiday with them. So she wrote a letter to Claire, and some time later Mr. and Mrs. Winters brought their little girl to the chalet, and left her there.

She was still in her long chair, but very happy to see Heidi again. Peter offered to push her out in her carriage, though of course they could not go up the mountain.

But then a wonderful thing happened! Claire's white cheeks

134

began to grow round and rosy. Then she found she could sit up. And after a while she could take a few steps, with Heidi and Peter holding her arms.

By the time her parents came to take her home, she could walk almost as well as ever. Mr. and Mrs. Winters wept when they saw this.

"It is a miracle! A miracle!" they cried, and they hugged and kissed Heidi.

They had to go home, of course, but Claire promised to come back and see Heidi again. And they wrote letters to each other. Heidi always signed hers, "From your friend Heidi, the happiest girl in the world."

The Little Mermaid

IN days long gone by, the King of the Oceans lived at the bottom of the sea in a fine palace, made of red coral, mother of pearls and shining shells.

The palace stood in the middle of a great stretch of sand and fine seaweed. In the distance, great brown rocks rose like hills, and green and brown seaweed grew around them like forests.

Here lived the folk of the sea; fish of many colours, lobsters and crabs with powerful claws, shell creatures of extraordinary shapes and hues – all coming and going.

The old king had five charming daughters who were mermaids. Each even more beautiful than the others, they all had long blonde hair that floated like seaweed, eyes as clear as the water, and graceful bodies that had fish tails instead of legs.

The girls lived quietly and happy in their undersea home, spending their time adorning themselves with jewellery which they made themselves from oyster pearls and coral and shells; or in such pleasant pastimes as singing, dancing, painting and weaving.

They all had nice manners. They were sweet and gentle, gay and joyful – oh, they were full of the joy of living. Their father loved all of them, but sometimes the youngest one worried him, for she was not quite like the others.

She seemed very dreamy, and not much interested in her world. Her sisters collected all kinds of rare seaweeds and sea plants and grew them in the garden which the king had given to each one of them. But the youngest one spent her time collecting thousands of bright yellow shells, which she arranged in a great pattern to look like the bright golden sun which shone on land, and which she had never even seen.

In the middle of this shell-sun she had placed a small statue of white marble which she had found on one of her lonely swims, in an old wreck lying at the bottom of the sea. The statue represented a very handsome young man – one from the land-world, where human beings lived.

And while her sisters made their jewellery, or danced and

sang with their friends, or searched for more pearls and more plants, or composed music to play on the harps they made from huge empty shells, the little mermaid passed whole days in her garden, just looking at the marble statue with a faraway expression, dreaming of the strange life which land-people must live. She could only guess what this life was like, but she did know that the people walked about on two legs, and she thought that must be quite marvellous.

At last her father said to her: "My child, why are you always alone and thinking, instead of singing and swimming with your sisters and their friends?"

"Father," she replied. "I keep thinking how wonderful it must be to live on the land-world where the beautiful sun always shines."

"Nothing of the sort!" said her father. "I can tell you that the climate on earth is far less pleasant than ours. Here the weather is always calm and even, but up there it is sometimes very cold and sometimes very hot, and people find it hard to protect themselves from the weather. Also, land-people are forced to work to earn their food, and sometimes the work is difficult and painful. Here in our kingdom there is all the food we want and we just help ourselves, without having to work all the time and sometimes even fight other people. Do you understand all that?"

"But perhaps if I went there I could find nice friends," she said.

Then he started to become angry.

"I see you don't understand! Now let me tell you this.

Land-people ... human beings ... find mermaids very ugly because they have fish tails instead of legs, and just because you look different from them, they don't want to know you."

The little mermaid wept.

"You are a very silly girl," he said severely. "And I forbid you even to go on thinking of such foolish things!"

But of course she did not stop thinking and dreaming about the land-people. It fascinated her, as mysterious and unknown things always fascinate people, and she secretly vowed that one day she would discover that world.

One of the customs of the sea-world was that when the mermaids reached their fifteenth birthday, they were allowed for the first time to swim to the surface of the sea.

And until that day, they dared not go up to the top.

Oh, how she longed for it!

Of course, all her elder sisters had had their fifteenth birthday and had been to the surface of the sea. The little mermaid did begin to spend more time with them, but only so that she found out things from them. She asked them endless questions.

They told her they had seen great ships sailing on top of the sea, thrusting their way through high waves as though they were nothing.

And if you went close enough to the land, they said, you could see wonderful towns full of splendid houses and streets.

"Tell me about the people," she begged. "Have you ever seen any?"

"Of course we have! Thousands of them! There are men, women and children, and they walk about on their two legs all the time."

"Not all the time," said another. "Sometimes they ride about in carriages drawn by strange creatures who have *four* legs – think of that, four legs, isn't it funny? They are called horses."

"And sometimes the people swim in the sea," said yet another. "At least they call it swimming. It's nothing like the real swimming that we can do. And that's very funny, too."

And she laughed gaily.

The little mermaid didn't think it was funny. To her it was all very astonishing, but sounded much more interesting than life down here. So free and happy. So many things to do. She was looking forward to it so much.

So she tended her shell-sun in her garden, and gazed at her statue and counted off the days.

And at last came that morning – her fifteenth birthday!

She left the palace very early without saying a word to anyone – her father, her sisters, or her servants. She held up her head, stretched her arms above them, and up, up, up she went!

And at last she reached the surface.

But it was still dark! And a terrible tempest was

raging. Thunder growled. Lightning flashed.

The wind howled wildly and lashed up horrific waves which were covered with thick black clouds. The waves made a terrifying sound which mingled with the noise of the thunder and howl of the wind.

It was very frightening for the little mermaid, who was only used to the calm and silence of the sea bottom, but she conquered her fear, and swam around easily, diving when the waves were too high and strong for her.

She could twist and turn like a fish in the water, and she was not going to let the storm stop her from reaching the shore, which was what she meant to do.

She became very tired indeed, but did not think of giving up.

Suddenly she heard a terrible noise near by, and through a break in the clouds, she saw a large ship just running aground on a jagged reef of coral. Oh, how sad, she thought, but there was nothing she could do. Sadly, she swam on.

Then a great flash of lightning lit up everything around her and she saw a piece of wreckage tossing by, and on it lay a young man, unconscious and badly hurt. An enormous wave was about to swallow him up.

"I must save him!" she cried.

Bravely she seized him and swam away with him, just as the wave dragged the wreckage down and under, out of sight forever.

The storm seemed to be dying now and it was becoming light. Far ahead of her she could see the shore.

142

There was no sign now of the ship that had been wrecked. She felt very lonely and tired and a bit unhappy, for this was not at all as she had thought it would be.

But now the shore was close, and with her last remaining strength she swam in to a quiet little beach, and laid the young man on the sand.

There he lay with his eyes closed, white, frozen, and looking ready to die.

The little mermaid knelt beside him. Oh, she wished she knew what to do! She gazed into his face, and saw that he was very handsome. She thought he looked very much like the marble statue in her sea-bottom garden.

All this time, as she stayed by him, the sky was getting lighter, and the storm had almost died away. Still the young man lay there.

Then a strange new brightness came into the sky, beautifully coloured like the mother-of-pearl of her shells. She looked out to sea, and there, on the horizon, the sun began to appear, great, golden – and warm!

It was beautiful, beautiful! Much more lovely than the shell-sun she had made. And warm, warm! She loved it. She clapped her hands together with joy.

At last she had seen the real sun, and felt its glorious warmth.

Now all she wanted was for the young man to recover. She leaned over him again. She smoothed his hair, and touched his face. She thought he did not seem so cold now. But of course, she thought, the sun was warming him up! And she remembered hearing somewhere that land-people could only live if they were warm.

With great difficulty she dragged him away from the rocks so that he was out of the shade, and so that the sun could reach him properly.

Still she watched. She could see that he was breathing. But he did not open his eyes.

If he would open his eyes and speak to her, she could ask him what she must do, and if she possibly could, she would do it.

If only she had legs and feet instead of just a tail, she would run and find someone to help. But she couldn't and she could see no one – nothing, in fact, except in the distance what looked like a palace.

Then she did see someone!

Coming down the path from behind the palace was a very pretty young lady. She was wearing beautiful clothes and she had long curly hair. And she had feet, with fine shoes on them!

She was coming this way!

Suddenly, the little mermaid felt very shy. So she ran and hid behind the rocks, watching as the lady came nearer and nearer.

And then the lady saw the young man lying there on the sand.

She began to run towards the young man.

The little mermaid, watching behind the rocks, saw the lady kneel down beside him and put her arm beneath his shoulders. Then she began to cry out, loudly:

"Help! Help!" she cried.

And from somewhere, two fishermen came running.

The mermaid saw them help him to his feet, and now she knew he was safe.

So she slipped quietly away back into the sea, and plunged downwards to her home.

But from that day on she never stopped thinking about the young man whose life she had saved. Now she spent even more time sitting in her garden, staring at her statue.

Sometimes she again made the jouney to the surface and swam ashore in the same spot where she had left him.

Once, hiding behind those same rocks, she overheard some fishermen talking between themselves.

And at last she learned that the handsome young man was none other than the ruling prince of this neighbourhood, and that he lived in that very same palace which she could still see in the distance.

And she also heard them talking about how the prince's ship had been wrecked in that great storm, and how the prince had been washed ashore, injured and unconscious. And how he might have died, except that he had been found lying there by a beautiful girl who had called for help, and had helped to take him back to his palace. And then she had disappeared, without telling anyone her name, or where she came from.

And ever since then, they said, the prince had been searching for her.

But no one said anything about a mermaid, who had rescued him from the sea.

When she heard this, the mermaid could not stop weeping.

"Tell me, child, what is making you so unhappy?" asked her father at last. "You weep and sit around. You know we love you, and only want to see you happy. My dear child, tell me what ails you."

Then she told her father all about her adventure on her fifteenth birthday, and said all she desired was to go and live on the land, and find the prince and stay somewhere near him for the rest of her life.

"Father," she begged. "I have heard of the witch who lives in the great hole behind the rocks, who can make magic and could change me into a human being. Please, father, let me go to her! I know I have deceived you and made you unhappy, but unless I can be near my beloved prince, I shall die!"

He was deeply shocked.

But she begged so hard that at last he agreed.

And off she went on a fearful journey, past the high rocks and down, down into a deep hole where the witch lived.

As soon as she arrived the witch croaked: "I know exactly why you have come. You want to be changed into a human being, a woman. Well, I can do it, but I warn you it will cost you a very high price."

"No price is too high to be near the prince whom I love," replied the mermaid. "Tell me what it is, and I will pay it."

"You must give me your beautiful voice," she said.

"Very well then, witch. Give me your potion, and I will give you my voice."

"Not so fast. You must pay in advance," said the witch.

The mermaid nodded. The witch came close. She said some strange, magic words, and made strange, magic signs.

And when the poor mermaid opened her mouth, no sound came from it. She was dumb!

Just for a moment she was afraid, then she remembered that very soon she would be a woman.

It took the witch three long hours to prepare the magic potion, but at last she came to the mermaid and gave her a crystal flask, in which there was a clear liquid.

"Take this flask," she said. "Swim up to the surface, and at the exact moment that the sun sinks from the sky, drink this liquid. It will turn your beautiful mermaid's tail into two legs like those of a human being. But I must tell you that you will suffer great pain while this is happening, and even afterwards, every step will be an agony."

"So think very well," she went on. "Be sure that what you are doing is right."

But the mermaid did not hesitate. She seized the flask. "What does it matter if I have no voice, and have to suffer a little pain?" she asked herself. "At least I shall be near my prince."

Without a backward look, or even a thought of her father, she flung herself up through the water. When she reached the little beach, she lay down on the sand, and as the sun sank from the sky, opened the flask and drank the liquid.

The pain began immediately. It lasted all through the night.

But when the sun rose again she awoke, and there, kneeling beside her, was the prince himself!

And as she looked down at herself, she saw that instead of her mermaid's tail, she now had two long, beautiful human legs!

The prince was looking at her with great kindness and sympathy. "I just came out for a walk and found you lying here," he said. "What is your name? Where have you come from?"

He seemed surprised that she did not answer, but of course, she could no longer speak.

She made signs to tell him that she was dumb, and at last he nodded. "I understand," he said. "You cannot speak. Oh, you poor girl! But come, let me take you to my palace. It is only a little way from here."

He helped her to her feet, but terrible pain shot through her legs and feet, as soon as she tried to walk.

"You are still faint," said the prince. "Come, let me help you."

He put his arm around her, and supported her all the way to his palace.

And there she stayed.

The prince gave her fine rooms and wonderful clothes and servants. There was everything to make her happy, and by sheer force of will, she overcame the pain in her feet and managed to act like a real woman.

She made herself dance, and this delighted the prince. And yet ... though he enjoyed her company, he did not love her. And one day, he told her about the lady he did love.

It was the beautiful girl who had found him on the beach after the little mermaid had rescued him from the sea.

He had never found her, he said. And he would never be able to love anyone else but her.

This made the poor little mermaid very unhappy, but she cheered up when the prince said he was going to visit the king of an island across the sea whom he had never met, and the mermaid was to go with him and his friends, to dance and play the harp for them.

It was a pleasant journey, but when they arrived, there beside the king was his beautiful daughter, and she was none other than the prince's unknown beloved!

Oh, how happy and overjoyed he was! Immediately

he asked the king if he might marry his daughter, and the king consented. There and then, a great, fine wedding was arranged.

The poor little mermaid thought she would die of grief after the wedding, for of course the prince no longer spent so much time with her, though he was still very kind to her.

The wedding festivities lasted a long time, but at last they prepared to sail home again, and the mermaid went with them.

Again she danced and played for everyone. But often now she was all alone, and then she would creep to the ship's side and stand there, looking out over the sea.

The beautiful sea, which she had given up for a foolish fancy which, she now saw, had brought her nothing but pain and anguish and deceit.

Standing there one night, all alone, she suddenly heard singing, and looking down at the sea, she saw her four dear sisters swimming around and calling to her.

"Dear sister, we have come to save you!" they called to her. "We have good news for you. We have seen the witch, and she has agreed to change you back into a mermaid! Yes! And all you have to do for her is to kill the prince who has made you so unhappy. She has given us this dagger to bring to you, and you must plunge it into his heart. Here you are – catch!"

They threw the dagger, and she caught it. "Quick! Quick!" they called to her.

She hurried to the prince's bedroom and crept in.

There he lay, beside his princess. She raised the dagger . . .

But she could not do it, for she loved him too much.

Then she went back on deck and threw the dagger overboard . . . . . and jumped in after it, though she knew she was no longer a real mermaid and could not live in the sea.

But as she jumped, thousands of twinkling lights appeared, and voices said: "Come with us, dear mermaid! We are the children of light, and we comfort all who have lived in sorrow."

She gave a happy cry, and drifted into their arms.